# The Storekeeper

a one hour novella...

adapted directly from the
Three Act Stageplay

written by

David R. Beshears

Greybeard Publishing
Washington State

Greybeard Publishing
P.O. Box 480
McCleary, WA 98557

email: publish.greybeardpublishing.com
Website:
www.greybeardpublishing.com

# The Storekeeper

# Chapter One

A wooden porch ran the width of the weathered storefront. The faded sign above the store read '*General Store*'.

On the porch was a wooden bench and an old, rickety rocking chair. A sign on the wall next to the screen door read '*Lunch Counter*', and at the corner of the building was a small sign with an arrow pointing behind the store that read 'To Trains'.

To one side of the store was a very old gas pump with an equally old sign: '*No Gas*'.

Mrs. Mayfield, an elderly black woman, sat primly in the rocking chair, gently rocking. She wore a clean but well-worn dress and clutched at a plastic purse that rested in her lap. Her hair, more gray than black, was pulled back and bound in a bun.

The Storekeeper sat on the bench next to the rocking chair, relaxed, one arm draped along the back of the bench. He was middle-aged, friendly and outgoing. He dressed casually, wore a flannel shirt with the sleeves rolled up.

The screen door opened and Wayne Saunders stepped out onto the porch, a bottle of cola in hand. Hinges screeched noisily as the screen door closed behind him.

"I put a pair of quarters on the counter," he said. He didn't sound all that pleased about it.

Wayne was thirty years old, rather disgruntled with a world that just wouldn't give him a break.

"I thank you, Mr. Saunders," said the Storekeeper.

"Yeah. Whatever." Wayne took a long pull on his cola, sighed tiredly as he looked out at the highway. "Ya' get many cars come by here?"

"Not a one."

"Doesn't that make it tough to earn a living?" asked Wayne. "Ya gotta have customers to run a store, don't ya'?"

The Storekeeper gave a slow nod. He wore a knowing, confident smile.

"You are here, Mr. Saunders," he said, matter-of-factly. "And you have made a purchase. That would make you a customer."

Wayne thought on that a moment, finally held the bottle up in salute.

"Glad to help, Storekeeper." He took another swallow of his cola, then looked over at Mrs. Mayfield. "So what's your story, lady?"

"I beg your pardon?" She didn't much like this man's tone.

"What brings you here? You a customer, too?"

All of Mrs. Mayfield's defenses went up. She clutched all the more tightly at her black, plastic purse. "I'm sorry, sir. I don't believe—"

"Oh, dear," said the Storekeeper, jumping in. "Where are my manners. Mrs. Mayfield, allow me to introduce Mr. Wayne Saunders. Mr. Saunders, this wonderful lady is Mrs. Mayfield."

"Mrs. Mayfield," Wayne nodded politely.

Mrs. Mayfield regained her composure. "Mr. Saunders."

The Storekeeper patted the back of the bench as he spoke, smiling at the lady in the rocking chair.

"Mrs. Mayfield is on her way to visit her sister," he said. "Isn't that right, Mrs. Mayfield?"

Mrs. Mayfield nodded sharply, curtly.

"That's right. Cecilia asked if I might stay with her for a spell. She's all alone, now that her husband Walter passed away." She eyed Wayne. She continued to maintain distance, but certainly didn't want to appear rude. "And you, Mr. Saunders?"

"Leavin' one city, headin' for another."

"I see." She thought on that. Her rocking slowed to an easy stop. She paused, then began rocking again, slow and steady. "That sounds sad."

The Storekeeper brought his arm down and sat forward. "I'm sure Mr. Saunders is simply seeking out new and exciting opportunities. Isn't that right, Wayne?"

"Exactly." Wayne went to what he knew best. "I'm not one to sit still. Heck no. Ya' gotta reach out and take life by the scruff a' the neck."

"Of course," said the Storekeeper.

"The system works against folks like me. The breaks are never gonna go my way all on their own." Wayne gave a crisp nod. "So I gotta work that much harder' everybody else."

"Make your own breaks, so to speak."

"Exactly."

"Good for you, Mr. Saunders," said Mrs. Mayfield, attempting to sound genuine.

She was also now finished with this particular conversation, having met whatever etiquette requirements may have been due here.

She returned her focus to her rocking.

"Yeah, well," Wayne grumbled. He finished his cola, looked around for where to dispose of the bottle.

The Storekeeper motioned to the screen door.

"The recycle bin is inside, sir; next to the pop cooler."

Wayne looked behind him, a hint of annoyance at having to take the empty back into the store and return it to right near where he got it to begin with.

He nonetheless opened the screen door and went inside.

Mrs. Mayfield glanced past the Storekeeper and to the door, as quickly returned her attention forward.

"That young man does have issues," she stated.

"Yes, he does, Mrs. Mayfield. Yes he does." He saw then a pair of new arrivals out on the highway. He smiled. "Ah. I believe this is the Harris couple."

Peter and Helen Harris were just starting onto the dirt and gravel parking lot, walking toward the storefront. They were in their twenties. Peter was dressed in light slacks and a short-sleeved button shirt. Helen was wearing summer shorts and a pullover blouse.

They warily eyed the two on the porch as they continued walking slowly toward the store. They appeared disoriented and were clearly out of their element.

"Maybe they can tell us…" Helen mumbled, let the thought fade.

"Maybe," said Peter. "Doubt it. Don't expect it would hurt to ask…"


Back on the porch, Mrs. Mayfield stopped her rocking yet again. She leaned forward just a mite as she looked in the direction of the newcomers.

"You know them?" she asked the Storekeeper.

"Oh, but of course."

Peter and Helen stopped at the foot of the porch steps. The Storekeeper gave a pleasant, welcoming nod and smile from his seated position on the bench.

"Hello, dear friends," he said.

Helen wore a lost gaze. "Hello."

"Yes," said Peter. "I uh… I think our car broke down."

"Of course it did," said the Storekeeper. "Of course it did."

Peter looked back toward the highway. "Out on… out on the uh… highway."

"We've been walking," said Helen.

"You poor dear," said Mrs. Mayfield.

Helen looked at Peter, who turned now from the highway and looked again up on the porch.

"Our car," he said.

"Our car," said Helen. "It broke down."

"I'm so sorry to hear that," said the Storekeeper. "Why don't you go on inside and get freshened up? It's a warm morning. And it's going to get warmer."

"Yes…" said Peter. "Sounds good."

Peter and Helen took the steps up onto the porch. As they approached the screen door, Helen smiled meekly at the Storekeeper.

"Yes," she said. "Thank you."

"My pleasure, Helen."

Helen hesitated, almost stumbled. The Storekeeper had spoken her name. She didn't remember telling him her name.

But Peter had already opened the screen door, drew her inside after him.

The screen door clattered noisily closed behind them.

Mrs. Mayfield leaned back in the chair and returned to her slow, comfortable rocking.

"Such a nice couple. And you say you know them?"

"Helen and Peter. Yes. A nice couple. Very nice."

"They seem a bit turned around."

"The long walk, no doubt," Storekeeper said thoughtfully.

"Yes, I'm sure you're right. They did say they had been walking a long time, didn't they?" She leaned forward then and looked in the direction from which the Harris couple had arrived a few moments earlier. "My, my. More company, looks like."

"Ah! How nice!" said the Storekeeper.

Molly Chandler crossed the empty dirt and gravel lot and approached the store. She was sixteen years old, but her eyes showed that she had seen more than the years would suggest. She wore faded jeans and a light jacket. She wore a knit cap, what hair was showing could have used a brushing.

She stepped to the foot of the steps, let a light backpack slide from her shoulder until she could set it at her feet.

The Storekeeper smiled broadly. "Good morning to you, Molly."

"Are you the Storekeeper here?"

"That would be me. And how are you this fine day?"

"I could use some water."

"You'll find the drinking fountain inside. Near the restrooms."

"Thanks." Molly picked up her backpack by a shoulder strap, climbed the steps up on onto the porch. She started toward the screen door. "I've been on the road for—"

She hesitated, as if she knew something, or thought she knew something; and then it was gone.

She stopped at the screen door, looked to the Storekeeper, over to Mrs. Mayfield.

"I've been walking…" she started again, hesitated again. "Been out… all morning…"

"The drinking fountain is inside," said the Storekeeper again.

"Right. By the restrooms."

"Exactly so."

"Yeah." Molly opened the screen door and went inside, hinges screeching, door clapping shut behind her.

Mrs. Mayfield returned to her easy rocking. "You recognized that poor girl. Molly, you said."

"Molly Chandler," said the Storekeeper. "Difficult time at home, I'm afraid. She's been on her own now for… well, for some time."

Mrs. Mayfield slowed her rocking, but didn't fully stop. "But… she didn't appear to know you."

"No, of course not," said the Storekeeper, quite matter-of-factly. "Why would she?"

"But…" Mrs. Mayfield was growing increasingly bewildered. "And the couple… they didn't—"

The screen door opened and Wayne came outside, cutting off Mrs. Mayfield's confusion. He looked curiously back inside as he let the screen ease closed.

"Hey, uh… Storekeeper. You may not get any cars passing by here, but you sure get a lot of foot traffic."

"It does look to be the day for it, doesn't it?"

"Kinda' odd, don't you think?" Wayne stepped to the edge of the porch, the top of the steps. "Way out here, middle a' nowhere, folks just walkin' up to your store?"

"Why would you think it odd, Wayne?"

Wayne looked a bit bewildered now himself. How could the Storekeeper not think…

"Cuz, you know… you're out here, in the middle of nowhere?"

"Nowhere, sir? Nowhere?"

"Well I—"

"I like to think of my little slice of paradise as the center of the universe."

Wayne looked back over his shoulder at the Storekeeper, still sitting on his bench.

"Really. You're kiddin', right?"

"I have an amazing sense of humor, Mr. Saunders, but when it comes to my world, I do not… *kid*."

"All right, all right. No need to get all tetchy on me."

The Storekeeper let a brief, thin smile show through. "Not at all, sir. Not at all."

There was an uncomfortable silence, broken only by the creaking of Mrs. Mayfield's rocker. She clutched more tightly at the plastic purse in her lap, gave an amiable nod.

"I find it very peaceful here," she said.

"No argument there, lady," said Wayne. "Quiet as a grave."

Storekeeper slid back on his bench, again rested an arm on the back. He gave a slight smirk. "Except for all that foot traffic?"

"Okay. Yeah. 'cept for that."

Mrs. Mayfield let out a pleasant sigh. "It feels like it's gonna be a warm one, though. Don't you think?"

"Exactly so, Mrs. Mayfield," said the Storekeeper.


Will Dawson stood at the far edge of the dusty parking lot, just off the asphalt of the highway. He watched the activity on the general store porch across the lot.

Will was in his thirties. He looked to be quite comfortable on his own. He had a tall walking staff in hand, wore black jeans and a light windbreaker, the style rather less contemporary than the clothing of Wayne Saunders and the Harris couple.

He glanced once up the highway to the distant horizon, then looked back at the store and the group gathered in the shade of the porch. He started across the gravel lot.

Wayne kept his attention on the figure walking slowly across the lot towards them, grumbled in the general direction of the Storekeeper.

"More foot traffic, Storekeeper. Cancel that *quiet as a grave*".

"That would be Will Dawson," said the Storekeeper.

Will approached the porch, planted a foot on the first step.

"Hello, folks."

"Good morning to you, Will," said the Storekeeper.

"Morning," Will said warily. "Do I know you?"

"I wouldn't think so."

"Then—"

"Mrs. Mayfield, Mr. Saunders, may I present William Dawson. An anthropologist, if I'm not mistaken. Did I get that right?"

"You seem to be not mistaken about a number of things, Storekeeper."

"It comes with the job, my friend."

"Uh, huh. Which would be?"

Storekeeper smiled warmly and indicated their surroundings. "Minding the store, of course."

Mrs. Mayfield ceased her rocking, leaned forward, back straight, and entered the conversation.

"Good morning to you, Mr. Dawson," she said calmly.

Will gave a nod of the head. "Mornin', ma'am. Please, call me Will."

Mrs. Mayfield shifted back again, and again returned to her slow, steady rocking, clutching her purse.

Obligations met.

Will acknowledged Wayne. "Mr. Saunders."

"*Will*... ya' been walking long?"

Will thought on that. He looked curiously in the direction he had traveled from, then turned back to Wayne.

"Some," he said. "I suppose."

There was another moment of uncomfortable silence. The Storekeeper was about to say something when he stopped himself. He hesitated.

He waited... one more moment.

There came the haunting sound of a train whistle in the distance. It faded, drifted... the Storekeeper smiled contentedly.

"It must be eight o'clock," he said.

Will doubted that. He knew for a fact that it was later than that. He reached into his pocket, pulled out an old pocket watch and looked at the time.

"It's nine thirty," he stated flatly.

"I'm pretty sure it's eight," said the Storekeeper.

Will held up his watch for all to see. "Never more'n a minute off, Storekeeper." He returned his watch to his pocket.

Issue settled.

Storekeeper shook his head. "Nonetheless, Will. It is eight o'clock. Here."

Will had no idea how to respond to that.

Wayne, meanwhile, lifted his hands in exasperation, quickly dropped them back to his side. "Oh, geez. What is that supposed to mean?"

"Just what I said, Wayne. No more, no less."

Wayne sighed loudly and turned to Will.

"He always talks like that."

"Do I?" asked the Storekeeper.

"Yes. You do."

As their exchange faded, Will took several steps to the left, used the head of his staff to indicate the 'To Trains' sign that hung on wall near the corner of the building.

"You have a train station back there, Storekeeper?"

"Of a sort. Up to now, the train has never had cause to stop."

"And it does now?" asked Will.

Storekeeper appeared to get a warm feeling all over…

"Soon enough, my friend. It will soon enough."

The little world of the general store again grew quiet. There wasn't even a breeze. No one spoke. For the moment no one moved.

Mrs. Mayfield had stopped her rocking. She leaned forward now and slowly stood up. With that, Storekeeper stood and walked to the screen door. He held it open for her. She entered the store, still clutching at her purse.

Storekeeper looked to Wayne, who decided to follow Mrs. Mayfield inside.

Storekeeper let the screen door close and returned to his bench. He indicated the empty rocking chair. Will Dawson climbed the steps up onto the porch. He sat in the chair, held the staff casually in front of him.

The two silently enjoyed the quiet of the warming morning.

## Chapter Two

The screen door opened with a screech and Storekeeper stepped outside. He had gone inside a few minutes earlier to see to his visitors, returned to his bench now and sat down.

"A dear, lovely lady, Mrs. Mayfield," he said.

Will Dawson was in the rocking chair. He shifted in the chair, leaned his staff against the wall.

"Yessir." He leaned forward, rested his elbows on his knees. "Storekeeper, I get the feeling that something just isn't right. And furthermore, I'm pretty sure that whatever it is that's going on, you are at the heart of it."

"All seems right enough to me, Will."

"See, now that's something right there," said Will, straightening again and looking over at Storekeeper. "You knew my name when I got here. You know me. How is that?"

"Why wouldn't I know you?"

"Because we've never met; because I've never seen you before."

"What does that have to do with it?"

"That." Will was increasingly frustrated. "What you just said. Ya' see, it makes sense. But it shouldn't make sense. None of this should make sense. None at all."

Will looked outward again, across the gravel parking lot, across the highway. It was all open fields and dry brush.

"There's stuff I should know," he said. "I know there's stuff I should know. There are… holes… in my mind. Empty places. I feel it. I'm not all here. I'm not… complete."

"Will Dawson, you are the most complete person here."

Will thought about that. He stood and stepped to edge of the porch. The world beyond the porch was still, was empty.

"Here," he sighed. "Yes sir, just where is that? Where is… here?"

"Here is the center of the universe, my friend."

Will turned his head and looked back at the Storekeeper.

"Your store. The center of the universe. Where it is always eight o'clock in the morning."

"Exactly so."

Will looked away again, frowned as he slowly shook his head in frustration.

"Sorry… I can't put my finger on it, but somehow that's wrong. Or, it should be wrong. That is wrong, where we are is wrong, and all of us… we are all so very wrong."

Storekeeper's cool, calm and collected sense of wellbeing remained strong. He stood up and stepped up beside Will.

"Do not be overly concerned, Mr. Dawson. All is well. Of all that you may doubt the world around you, I believe you know that you can trust me." He gave Will a gentle smile. "Is that not so?"

Will spoke without looking at his host. "What I believe is that you are smack-dab in the middle of what's going on. Trust you? Let us say that I have some concern when it comes to your motives. I should probably fear you. We all should fear you."

"And yet you do not fear me."

"No," Will mumbled softly. "I don't."

"That is good. As for my motives," Storekeeper's eyes grew just a little bit brighter. "They are brimming over with good intentions."

"Uh, huh. We'll see." Something in the distance caught Will's eye. He saw then a woman standing at the far edge of the lot. "More company. Why am I not surprised?"

"And so," said the Storekeeper, sounding quite satisfied. "We are all here."

Edie Paulsen started across the lot toward them. She was about thirty years old, but looked worn, as if life had beaten her down. Her clothes had been nice at one time, but now appeared as worn out as their owner.

"Excuse me," she said as she drew near. "I think I'm lost."

"Hello, Edie," said the Storekeeper comfortingly. "No need to worry. You are exactly where you need to be."

Edi looked at the store, then at Will, then back at the Storekeeper.

"I am?"

"You certainly are, my dear."

Edie again looked slowly over at Will. Will gave her a friendly nod.

"Will Dawson. And I am as confused as you are."

"I seriously doubt that."

"Will Dawson, this is Edie Paulsen," said Storekeeper. "Edie, meet Will Dawson."

"Hey," said Edie unenthusiastically.

"Nice to meet you," said Will.

"If you say so." Edie looked around her, behind her, back again to the two gentlemen on the porch. She took a step to one side, then another. She looked up at the sign that read 'To Trains'.

She looked pointedly then at the Storekeeper.

"Are we dead?"

This got Will's attention. He looked sharply at Storekeeper, quite interested to hear the Storekeeper's response.

The Storekeeper, for his part, was genuinely surprised at such a question.

"Oh, my no," he stated. "Absolutely not. What would make you think such a thing?"

"I don't know how I got here. I don't know where here is. And I don't know where I was before I was here."

"Yeah…" said Will. "Neither do I."

For the first time that morning, Storekeeper looked flustered. "Now you two stop all this foolishness. You are most definitely not dead. This isn't heaven. Or hell. Or anything of the sort."

"The center of the universe?" Will asked slyly.

"Exactly so. Yes. Exactly so." Storekeeper felt once again on familiar ground. "Welcome. Welcome to the center of the universe."

Edie pointed to the 'To Trains' sign.

"With train service."

"For you, my dear? Most certainly. Train service."

"For me," Edie said coolly. "Train service."

"Exactly so."

"To where?"

Will wanted the answer to that as well. "Yeah, Storekeeper. Just where does this eight o'clock train go?"

"Where does it go?" Storekeeper stumbled a moment in his thoughts. He grew introspective. When he spoke again, it was as if to himself. "It goes wherever we want it to go, wherever we need it to go. Wherever we take it, that is where it will take us. It goes to grand worlds, fantastical lands; to wondrous sights and sounds and dreams."

Will looked accusingly at Storekeeper.

"You don't know. Do you? It's the one thing –the only thing—that you don't know."

Storekeeper shrugged. "No one knows where the train goes. How can we? We haven't gone there before. So we can't know. Not until we get there."

"Am I going?" asked Edie. "On the train?"

"I would say that's a safe bet, Edie," the Storekeeper said confidently. "I can't say with absolute certainty, but it is a fairly safe bet." He looked to Will. "And I'm figuring you, as well. Most likely, most likely."

Storekeeper moved over to the screen door, opened it to the accompanying sound of screeching hinges.

"How about we go inside? Maybe have bite to eat? Sandwiches?"

"Sure. Why not," said Will. He held a hand down to Edie. "Miss Paulsen?"

Edie took the offered hand and took the steps up to the porch.

"Why not?" she asked. "I can't say as I remember when I ate last."

Will allowed Edie to go inside first. She passed by the Storekeeper, who gave her a welcoming nod.

Once alone on the porch, Storekeeper took a moment to look around. He smiled pleasantly, gave another slow, easy nod, then followed Will and Edie inside.

# Chapter Three

Storekeeper stood behind a small lunch counter that ran along one wall, the sign behind him reading 'Sandwiches'. His arms rested on the counter-top, his focus on the others in his store.

There was a checkout counter with cash register near the screen door that led outside. Out on the floor were two small tables, each with three chairs. Beyond the tables was a single row of store shelves six-feet long containing boxed and canned goods.

On the wall beside a hallway leading to the back of the store was what appeared to be the very same 'To Trains' sign that had been posted outside.

Wayne Saunders sat on one of the stools at the lunch counter. He faced away from the Storekeeper, his elbows on the counter behind him.

Mrs. Mayfield sat at one of the two tables, her ever-present purse in her lap. Peter and Helen sat at the table with her.

Will Dawson, Molly Chandler and Edie Paulsen sat at the other table.

Everyone had either a soda pop or a cup of coffee near to hand. A few had what remained of their sandwiches.

Wayne looked keenly at Edie.

"Say, Edie… it is Edie, right? I know you. Don't I?"

Edie lifted her pop bottle to her lips and took a drink. She set the bottle back onto the table.

"I don't think so."

"Sure I do. Yeah, I'm just about positive. I have definitely seen you somewhere." He thought on that a moment, and then another moment. "Chicago. Yeah. You been to Chicago?"

Edie glanced up at Wayne for the first time, then looked casually over at Will and Molly, then down at her soda.

"Sorry. I don't think I've heard of the place."

"Yeah, right," chuckled Wayne.

Molly, sitting at the table beside Edie, furrowed her brow. "Chicago… it's back east, right?"

"What? No. You guys are messin' with me, right? Chicago… Windy City? Chi-Town? Heart of America?" Wayne looked from one face to another throughout the room. "The Big Onion?"

Blank stares looked back at him. He quoted from the song then, almost but not quite singing:

"My Kind of Town, Chicago Is?"

More blank stares.

"Of course, Wayne," said Storekeeper. "Chicago."

Mrs. Mayfield smiled sympathetically. "Yes, Mr. Saunders. Chicago. A wonderful city."

"Right," Wayne droned.

Will appeared to be mulling it over.

"Yes," he said hesitantly. "Al Capone. A gangster."

"Really?" asked Molly.

"I think so."

Wayne grew more flustered by the moment. "What is the matter with you people?"

"Well, it has been quite the long day, Mr. Saunders," said Mrs. Mayfield.

Will couldn't help himself. "Mrs. Mayfield, haven't you heard? It's only eight o'clock in the AM."

"Yes, of course." Mrs. Mayfield sounded uncertain. "That's right. I'm so sorry. My mistake."

"Now you're getting' it," said Storekeeper.

"Did I miss something?" asked Peter.

"Probably," Will said flatly. "I know I have."

Wayne shook his head doggedly as he turned about on the stool and leaned forward onto the lunch counter, facing the Storekeeper.

"I give up."

Storekeeper remained ever upbeat. "Don't be so downhearted, Wayne. It's not so bad. Trust me."

"Why?"

"Oh, Mr. Saunders, you are the Gloomy Gus, aren't you?" He looked past Wayne to those sitting at the two tables. "Did everyone get their fill?"

Mrs. Mayfield held up the last small piece of her sandwich.

"Why, yes. Thank you, sir," she said. "Thank you very much. I hadn't realized how famished I was."

"My pleasure, Mrs. Mayfield."

Mrs. Mayfield set the bit of sandwich down onto the open paper napkin that was spread on the table in front of her.

She brushed her hands together to wipe away any remaining crumbs, looked across the table at Peter and Helen Harris.

"It was quite tasty. Don't you think?"

"Yes it was," said Helen. "It was very good."

"Yes, very good," Peter said absently. He looked curiously at the elderly woman. How had she ended up out here in the middle of nowhere? "Mrs. Mayfield, have you been on the road long? Traveling, I mean?"

Mrs. Mayfield put on a straight, slight smile, empty, with nothing behind it. Her words were mechanical, the tone oft-repeated, the statement verbatim what she had said earlier.

"Cecilia asked if I might stay with her for a spell. She's all alone, now that her husband Walter passed away."

"I see," said Peter. "That's where you're headed, then? To Cecilia's?"

"Yes. Cecilia. My sister. She asked if I might stay with her for a spell."

"Right..." said Peter. This was getting awkward. Still, he pushed on. "Where does your sister live?"

"Cecilia? My sister?" Mrs. Mayfield nervously straightened and re-straightened the napkin spread out in front of her. "I... um..."

She delicately pushed aside the napkin and the remaining bit of sandwich. She brought her black, plastic purse up from her lap, placed it meticulously on the table in front of her. She clutched at it protectively.

"Oh, dear. Isn't this something?" There was a hint of fear in her voice. "I'm afraid it's gone completely out of my head for the moment. Flew away. Just like that. I am so sorry."

"That's all right, Mrs. Mayfield," said Helen. "It's not important. Really."

"Oh dear, oh dear."

Helen's tone grew light, conversational. "So, where are you from, then?"

"The south," said Mrs. Mayfield, quick and certain. "I'm from the south."

"Is that right?" Helen's smile was slightly forced. "The south, you say?"

"That's right." She lifted her purse from the table and placed it back down onto her lap. "Yes. I'm from the south."

"That's nice. That's... that's really, really nice." Helen looked nervously to Peter. "Isn't that nice, Peter?"

"Yeah, sure," said Peter. "Nice."

Mrs. Mayfield nodded curtly and gave Peter and Helen a wry wink. A final sharp nod and then...

The conversation was concluded.

Mrs. Mayfield was done.

Peter rested a comforting hand on Helen's arm.

"How about we take a breath of air?"

"Yes. I think that would be... just splendid." Helen looked to Mrs.

Mayfield. "Would you excuse us, Mrs. Mayfield?"

Mrs. Mayfield gave a dismissive nod. Peter and Helen took that as a yes. As they started toward the door, Wayne spun slowly around on his stool.

"I have a short journey of my own to take." He slipped off the stool and headed toward the back of the store, past the 'restrooms' sign and into the hallway.

Will Dawson stood up from the table then, picked up his cup and walked casually to the lunch counter. He set the cup down and slid it toward Storekeeper.

"Another again, barkeep, and don't be stingy with the caffeine."

"As you will, kind sir."

The Storekeeper reached below the counter, brought up a coffee carafe and refilled Will's cup.

There came then the haunting sound of a distant train whistle.

"Eight o'clock, then?" asked Will.

"Exactly so."

"And… it's always eight o'clock."

"Right."

Will reached down for his cup. "And, you don't find anything odd about that…"

"Not at all," said Storekeeper. "It's eight o'clock. Therefore, it is eight o'clock."

Will gave a slight salute with his coffee cup as he turned back to return to his table.

"An odd universe you have here, Storekeeper."

"I take that as a compliment, Mr. Dawson."

"That… is not a surprise."

# Chapter Four

Will sipped at his coffee, leaned back in his chair and studied the 'To Trains' sign that hung on the wall beside the hallway. It looked exactly the same as the sign outside.

He spoke to Storekeeper, still standing behind the lunch counter.

"You say there's a train station behind your store… it's through there?"

"It's not far. Quite a lovely place."

"I don't recall seeing it."

"No need to see it just yet. But soon. We'll head over there soon."

This was the first Molly had heard of this.

"We're taking a train?" she asked, not to anyone in particular.

Edie held her bottle of pop up before her.

"So the man says." She took a drink, set the bottle back on the table. Did you have plans to take a train ride today, Molly?"

"I, uh—"

"I didn't think so. I know I didn't. Not that I can remember. But then, I really don't remember much of anything."

"I, uh… train?" Molly looked anxious. "I don't have any money." She repeated to the Storekeeper. "I don't have any money."

"Not to worry, sweetheart," said the Storekeeper. "Train fare is on the house."

"Thank you. That's very nice of you." Apprehensively then, "Where are we going?"

Will snickered lightly at that, recalling the answer that he got when he had asked that same question earlier.

"Yes, Storekeeper," he said. "Please, do tell the young lady where we are going."

Storekeeper smiled warmly, not offended in the slightest at Will's light jab.

"We'll know when we get there, Molly." Storekeeper gave a sharp nod. "We will surely know when we get there."

Mrs. Mayfield perked up, clutching at her purse.

"I was on a train once. With my Herbert." She wore a nostalgic smile. "Oh, so many years ago. We took the train to… oh, dear. I'm not sure now just where. It was a pleasant trip. Yes. Though it was an awfully hot day. I do remember that. And the bologna sandwiches we brought with us? They were very warm. You know how bologna sandwiches can get."

She retreated back into her thoughts then, and the others grew politely silent.

The quiet was broken only when Peter and Helen came back through the screen door. Peter had his cell phone in hand. He spoke to those in the room, to no one in particular, as he and Helen continued to their table with Mrs. Mayfield.

"No signal," said Peter. "I mean, nothing at all."

"Oh, no, no, no, Peter," said Storekeeper. "You won't be able to use that here. Oh, my no."

Molly looked curiously at the strange object in Peter's hand as Peter and Helen settled in at the other table.

"What is that?" she asked.

"My phone," Peter said absently.

"Your what?"

"Phone." Peter held it up. "You know... *phone*?"

"Really? Your own phone?"

"Uh, yeah..."

"Can I see it? Do ya' mind?"

"Yeah, sure." Peter leaned over and handed Molly his phone. "Just a lousy phone. Nothing fancy."

Molly admired the phone without fully comprehending it. Peter had turned back to his table.

"And apparently totally useless here, in the center of the universe." He looked over at the Storekeeper. "Do you have a landline I can use?"

"I'm sorry, Peter. There really isn't much use for one here."

"Don't know about that. I could use one 'bout now."

Storekeeper looked sympathetically over at Peter. "And just who would you call, my friend?"

"Well, I was going to call… uh—" Peter was suddenly uncertain, confused. "I, uh… well, I was…"

He looked pleading over at Helen. "Help me out here, Helen. Who was I going to call?"

"I don't know," said Helen. "I don't remember."

Peter looked lost. "A minute ago I was… now for the life of me, I can't remember."

Molly handed the phone back to Peter.

"How does it work?" she asked.

Peter stuffed the phone back into his pocket. "Didn't you hear? It doesn't."

"What doesn't?" Wayne came in from the hallway, walked across to the lunch counter.

"His own personal phone," said Molly.

At that, Wayne lost interest real fast. "Yeah. Ain't that just a real shocker."

"Probably cuz it's not connected up to anything."

Wayne chuckled lightly as he slid onto the stool.

"No doubt." He looked across the counter to the Storekeeper. "So, what's the plan, Stan?"

"The plan?" Storekeeper held his head back and thought on that. "Well, such as there is a plan, I suppose it would be simply that we will all soon walk over to the station in anticipation of the train's arrival."

"Good plan, good plan." Wayne parsed the Storekeeper's statement in his mind, curled his brow and frowned. "Somebody going on a trip?"

"We all are," said Molly.

"Is that so," said Wayne, looking over his shoulder at Molly.

"We can only hope," said the Storekeeper.

Edie shifted in her chair and folded her arms on the table. "What's that supposed to mean?" she asked. "Are we going to the train station or not?"

"Oh, my yes, Edie," said the Storekeeper. "We're all going to the station. That is why you are here. That is why you have all come to my store, to… the center of the universe."

"If that's so," said Edie, "Then what do you mean, we can only hope?"

"Excuse me?"

"You said a moment ago; we can only hope that we are all going."

Storekeeper continued his increasingly annoying knowing manner as he provided his easy yet thoughtful response.

"Ah. Yes. We draw nearer that moment in the great narrative when the determination will be made; the epochal decision that awaits each one of us. Each one of you." He paused, held a hand absently before him. "We shall all go the train station. We shall all be there when the train arrives at the gate. Of that, I am certain. I have no doubt. But as to who is to board that train? That I cannot with certainty say."

"Why not?" asked Molly.

"Because I don't know, dear girl. The decision has not yet been made."

Wayne looked sharply across the counter at their host. "What the heck are you talkin' about, Storekeeper?"

Storekeeper took a long, thoughtful pause, and when he spoke again, it was with considerable patience.

"In the story that has been your life, you have always known all that you needed to know in order to take each next step. Have you not?"

"Well, I—"

"Oh, you may have had doubts, concerns, questions, but in the end, you were able to take that step; at each and every critical moment."

"I suppose," Wayne said softly, rather uncertainly.

Storekeeper grew more somber. His tone was suddenly more serious than it had ever been.

"That is the way of it, Mr. Saunders. It always has been. For you..." He spoke then to the entire group gathered in his general store. "For all of you. You are truly unique. Truly. And so… the next step will come when it will come. For each of us. For each of you. It most certainly will."

He lifted his gaze upward. A few seconds later, there came again the haunting sound of the train whistle in the distance.

The Storekeeper waited for the train to pass, the sound to fade.

"Let us make our way to the station, my friends," he said.

Wayne turned about and slid off the lunch counter stool. "Heck, might as well. Curiouser and curiouser we go." He approached the tables, stopped behind Edie and held her chair as she slid back. "Miss Paulsen."

"Thank you," she said. She and Wayne continued to the hallway and were gone.

Storekeeper stepped around the lunch counter and approached the tables. "Folks?"

Will looked across the table.

"Molly? Shall we?" They stood and followed Wayne and Edie into the hallway.

Storekeeper stood before the other table. Mrs. Mayfield appeared quite calm, but Peter and Helen looked a bit anxious.

"How about you folks?" he asked.

"The train?" asked Helen. "Do you really think this is necessary?"

"Absolutely, Helen. It is, after all, the reason you are here."

"It is?" asked Peter. He sounded almost accusatory. "How can you know that? I mean, how can you know for sure that's why we're here?"

"There can be no other reason. You are here, you have come here, you will go now to the station, because you are… you. Each of you… you are… you."

Helen looked uneasily across at Peter. He reached out and took her hand.

"Helen," he stated, attempting calm. "We might as well."

Helen struggled to come to terms with it. She didn't even know why she was apprehensive, but she was. The train station meant something… important. Their lives would change there, and she didn't know that she was ready for what that change might be.

She finally took a long, shaky breath.

"All right." She stood, slowly. Peter stood with her and led her to the hallway.

"Good. Very good," said the Storekeeper. He focused his attention now on Mrs. Mayfield. He pulled one of the now-empty chairs to him and sat facing her.

"Mrs. Mayfield? How are you doing?"

"I'm doing just fine, sir," she said. "How about yourself?"

"I couldn't be better; not an ounce better. Are you ready to join the others?"

"Oh, I don't know. I was thinking I might just stay here. I mean, after all, I haven't even finished my coffee and sandwich."

"Dear Mrs. Mayfield." He gave his most compassionate smile. "I couldn't let you do that."

"Oh, you go on ahead, son. I'll be fine." She tried an amusing smile. "I promise not to steal anything."

"Mrs. Mayfield..."

Mrs. Mayfield looked away from Storekeeper. Her expression turned knowing, as did her tone.

"I don't imagine it will take long. When the time comes. Do you?"

"No," Storekeeper said softly. "No, I'm sure it won't."

"Well then, I'll just sit right here until it's over."

"No, ma'am. I can't let you do that." Storekeeper manner turned more determined. "Your presence is required at the train station."

Mrs. Mayfield looked directly at Storekeeper.

"Sir?"

"You will be on that train when it leaves."

"D'you really think so?"

"I most certainly do." He stood then, held out a hand for Mrs. Mayfield.

She looked up into Storekeeper's kind face. She smiled warmly and took the offered hand.

"Well, if we must."

"Yes, ma'am."

# Chapter Five

The Storekeeper stood behind the ticket window. He now wore a black suit coat and a cap on his head. A sign beside the ticket window read 'Southbound 8:00 AM'.

A long, worn wooden passenger waiting bench near the center of the room faced the ticket window. Mrs. Mayfield sat at one end of the bench, her purse in her lap. Edie and Molly sat together at the other end.

A sign over an arched opening read 'Gate 1'. Hanging on the wall beside the gate was the familiar 'To Trains' sign.

Peter and Helen were standing on the platform beyond the gate, their backs to the gate. They appeared to be watching for the train.

Will came through the gate and into the station. He stepped up to the ticket window and rested an elbow on the counter. He looked from the group on the bench to the Storekeeper and back.

"Wayne is out there putting pennies on the track," he said.

Molly had never put pennies on tracks before, but she had heard of it. The train flattens the pennies as it rolls over them.

"How is he going to collect them if he's going with us?"

"That's what I asked him," said Will. He shrugged. "He said he'd have time."

Edie looked to the Storekeeper with the hint of a smirk.

"What do you say to that, Storekeeper? Will he have enough time? Maybe all the time in the world?"

"If you mean is he going to be on the train when it leaves, I really couldn't say, Edie. Not for certain. Not just yet."

"Not just yet? Well that's downright intriguing. You don't know yet, but you will? Are you saying that you <u>will</u> know who is going and who isn't?"

Storekeeper responded with a tip of his hat.

"I wear the hat of ticket agent now, Miss Paulsen. The ticket agent usually knows who's getting on the train."

"But... shouldn't we all go?" asked Molly, increasingly anxious. "Shouldn't we all get on the train?"

Edie shifted about on the bench, continued to look at Storekeeper as she answered Molly's question for him.

"The decision is out of our hands," she said, then spoke directly to Storekeeper. "Isn't that right, Storekeeper?"

"Exactly so."

"But it's not in <u>your</u> hands, either. Is it?"

"No, ma'am. It certainly is not."

"And you don't know where the train is going," said Edie, an observation, not a question.

"I expect we won't know that until it gets there."

"Yes. So you said."

"Yes, ma'am. That I did."

Molly scooted forward, stood slowly. "I don't want to be left behind."

Edie reached out and placed a hand gently on Molly's arm.

"It's all right, sweetie. I'm sure you'll be going."

"You don't know that." Molly looked from Edie back to the Storekeeper. "You don't know that."

"No," stated Storekeeper. "I don't."

"Don't you worry, dear," said Mrs. Mayfield. "Comes to that, I'll stay here with you."

Storekeeper spoke tolerantly. "That's very thoughtful of you, Mrs. Mayfield. But you know very well that's not how it works."

This comment by Storekeeper made just about everyone mighty curious. Will was the one who spoke up.

"Mrs. Mayfield?" he asked. "You know how this works?"

Mrs. Mayfield hesitated, thought on what the answer might be.

"Quite odd, really," she said at last. "I think so. Not that I could put any of it into words, mind you, but there's things spinnin' round in my head. Bits o' knowledge and curiosities; I've no idea how any of it got there. But it's all there just the same." She frowned and sighed. "I just can't seem to wrap my head 'round any of it. Seems, more I focus, the more it slips away."

"I'm really sorry to hear that," said Will. He turned sharply to Storekeeper. "I'll bet you could, though, couldn't you? Wrap your head around it? You got your head wrapped around it?"

"What I need to know comes to me when I need to know it, Will. I cannot reach out for it. It must come to me."

Mrs. Mayfield spoke as if from a daydream, soft and distant.

"It's like shadows in a mist." She glanced up to the others. "If you try to make out the shapes, they fade to gray."

Her words hung there in empty space for several long seconds. The Storekeeper finally broke the silence.

"Just so, Mrs. Mayfield. Exactly so."

Another several moments of silence. Molly took a stumbling step backward. "I'm gonna go outside." She turned and started toward the gate.

Edie stood and followed after her.

"I'll go with you Molly. I seem to recall that I enjoy standing at the tracks, watching for the train." She grumbled then as she went through the gate. "Not that I remember actually seeing tracks… or a train…"

Once beyond the gate, Edie turned left and continued after Molly. Peter and Helen, still standing near the tracks, turned at the movement and seeing them, followed them.

Will, still at the counter, turned to Storekeeper, standing on the other side of the counter.

"Well, Storekeeper… *Mr. Ticket Agent.* You appear to be frightening off the clientele."

"Not to worry, Will. All shall be right enough before the train gets here." He glanced to his right. He saw something on the counter that wasn't there before. "Ah! Here we go. So it begins in earnest."

He picked up the brochure-sized piece of paper. It was a train ticket. He took an envelope sleeve from a stack on the counter and slipped the ticket into the sleeve.

"Waddya have there, Storekeeper?" asked Will.

Storekeeper ignored the question. He stepped from behind the counter and approached Mrs. Mayfield. He took up position directly in front of the woman, gave a half-bow.

"Madam, I have your ticket."

"Oh, my. Do you really?"

"Yes, ma'am." He handed her the ticket. "And here you are."

"Oh, dear." She clutched at the ticket. "Oh dear, oh dear. Thank you."

"Not at all. You enjoy your journey."

Will waited impatiently as Storekeeper returned to his place behind the counter.

"Is that how this is going to go?" he asked. "We'll find out who's taking the train one at a time, whenever you feel like handing out a ticket?"

"I will distribute the tickets as they come to me."

"Come to you? You—"

"As they come to me," Storekeeper stated calmly.

"You tryin' to tell me you don't have the tickets back there waiting to be handed out?"

"As tickets are made available, I will present them to those named on the ticket."

Will gave the Storekeeper a long, thoughtful study.

"You are the odd one, Storekeeper."

"Yes, I suppose that is so." Storekeeper grinned. "But then, as you have already observed, I live in an odd universe."

At that moment, Wayne appeared in the gate portal and came into the station.

"You most certainly do," he said. He approached the counter, leaned an elbow on the countertop. "So, I've been talkin' with that kid. What's her name? Molly? Ya' know she's never seen a television? She's never even heard of 'em."

"That's kinda odd," said Will. "I know a lot a' motel rooms got 'em nowadays. You'd a thought she would a—"

"What?" Wayne cut him off. "That's not the…"

Wayne can't even finish the thought. What the heck's going on here?

Storekeeper smiled patiently. "It's not really all that surprising, Wayne. We each walk through our own individual worlds, live our lives through individual experiences."

"You can paint it with all the philosophizing you want, Storekeeper. She should know from televisions. And now I think on it, she looked at that couple's cell phone like it was magic."

This brought to the forefront Will's own questions, though for slightly different reasons. He started to say something, but in the end waved the thoughts away.

Wayne noticed the odd expression on Will's face.

"Yeah?" he urged.

"Nevermind."

"Sure," said Wayne. He looked carefully at Will. He thought about the group gathered here. Molly, Will, Edie... "Say... buddy. I'm getting an idea here."

"And?"

"Tell me, what year is it?"

"Year?"

"Simple. What year is it?"

"I, uh..."

"You tellin' me you don't know what year it is?" Wayne looked over at the Storekeeper. This went even deeper than he first thought. "Okay, so you tell me how he doesn't know what year it is."

"Will doesn't know what year it is because the year has never been an issue for him."

"What?" Wayne sounded incredulous.

The look in Will's eyes could have been fear.

"Storekeeper... I told you. I told you..." Will's words were soft, lost. "I have... empty places... in my mind. I should know what year it is. I told you. There's stuff I should know that I don't know."

"My friend," said the Storekeeper. "In all the story that has been your life, what importance the year? Has the subject ever come up? It has not. What matter does it have now?"

Will slowly shook his head. "No... don't start twisting this around like it doesn't matter. It should have come up. It should have." He leaned against the counter. "It should have come up. Shouldn't it? At some point, some time? Sometime in my life?"

"Of course it should have!" said Wayne. "What kinda' crazy talk is this?" He worked his way over to the long bench and plopped himself down. He rested his arms on the back of the bench.

"Okay. Let's think this through. We gotta be on drugs or something." He pointed at the Storekeeper. "That guy is messing with our minds. It's some kind of experiment."

"Mr. Saunders, I—"

"So, are you a scientist or a doctor or something?"

"No. No, I'm just a storekeeper." He indicated their current surroundings. "And, on occasion, a ticket agent, it would seem."

The Storekeeper glanced to his right a second time. There was another ticket on the counter. He reached out and picked it up.

"Here we go." He slipped the ticket into a sleeve, held it out to Will. "Mr. Dawson. Your ticket, sir."

Will took the ticket, looked at it, only half comprehending.

Mrs. Mayfield smiled openly. "Well, isn't that nice."

Will stared numbly at the ticket. "I'm going then."

"Yes, sir," said Storekeeper. "It looks that way."

"D'you ever doubt it?" smirked Wayne.

"Yes, actually."

"I didn't," said Wayne. "You always struck me as one of the surviving characters." He rested his elbows on his knees. "The way I'm seein' it, some of us are gonna survive this thing, some of aren't. You are one of the survivors. I saw that right from the start."

"I don't understand."

Storekeeper spoke evenly. "Mr. Saunders, a lot of protagonists fail to live through their own stories."

"That may be, but we're <u>all</u> protagonists here, aren't we?"

The Storekeeper was taken aback at Wayne's observation. This young man had seen something.

"That is very perceptive, Mr. Saunders. I believe you are… almost… correct."

"Almost, huh?"

"I believe so."

"Yeah, well, we may not all be the hero, but we each come from our own story."

"Isn't that always the case, Wayne?"

Wayne shook his head tiredly, again leaned back and placed his arms on the back of the bench.

"No, Storekeeper. You're not gonna get by using slippery words this time. I'm startin' to get a handle on this thing, and you know it."

Mrs. Mayfield shifted nervously. The conversation was making her uncomfortable.

"I believe I'll step outside for a bit."

"Of course, Mrs. Mayfield," said Storekeeper.

"Let me, ma'am." Will stepped forward and assisted Mrs. Mayfield to her feet.

"Very kind of you, Will." She slipped an arm through Will's offered elbow and the two stepped to the gate and out onto the platform just as Helen and Peter entered the station.

The Storekeeper placed two tickets into sleeves. "Excellent timing, you two," he said.

"Excuse me?" asked Peter.

Storekeeper stepped around the counter, and with some flair handed them their tickets. Peter and Helen sat down on the bench and Peter patted Helen's hand.

Wayne looked down the bench to them. They looked as bewildered as ever.

"Well, well. Congratulations."

They nodded uncertainly, Peter mumbling an awkward thank you.

Wayne returned his attention to the Storekeeper. "We're coming down to it, eh?"

Storekeeper appeared even more thoughtful than usual. He studied Wayne with a curious gaze, held it for an uncomfortable moment.

"It would seem so," he said quietly.

Wayne found Storekeeper's unexpected response really, really unsettling.

"Right," he finally managed.

# Chapter Six

Edie came in from the platform. "Sweet kid, that Molly. If she isn't on that train…"

Storekeeper held up a hand and frowned.

"As I said, Miss Paulsen. I—"

"Yes, yes, I know what you said."

The Storekeeper's smile returned then. He began putting together another packet.

"Ah. Miss Paulsen, I have your ticket."

Edie moved awkwardly to the counter. She stared down at the ticket.

"If Molly isn't—"

"I am sorry," said Storekeeper. "I can't say."

Edie used a finger to push the ticket about on the counter.

"It is a relief, I suppose. Though for the life of me, I couldn't tell you why."

"I would think it obvious," said Wayne, still sitting on the bench. "Because it is for the life of you."

Edie took the ticket and turned about, gave Wayne a stern glare.

"What would make you say such a thing?"

"Just what do you think is going to happen to anyone left behind? Might this poor lost soul simply walk out of here? To where?"

"I couldn't say."

"It had to cross your mind. You're the one that mentioned the kid." He shifted his gaze from Edie to the Storekeeper, back again to Edie. "Let's make it a bit more personal yet. If you hadn't been given a ticket, where would you go once the train pulled out of the station, leaving you standing out there on the platform waving bye-bye?"

"I don't know," she managed.

"No, of course you don't."

"How can I? How can any of us?"

Wayne smiled. "My point."

Edie was done with this. She turned away from Wayne, moved around behind the bench.

"Excuse me," she said, speaking in the general direction of the Storekeeper as she looked about the station. "Where is the, uh…"

Storekeeper pointed to a narrow hallway. "Right through there, Miss Paulsen."

She left quickly then, leaving only Storekeeper and Wayne in the station.

"There was no need to upset Miss Paulsen," said Storekeeper. "She has her ticket, after all."

"Yes. And that leaves just me and the girl now, doesn't it? How many you figure are going to be stayin' on here after the train leaves the station, Storekeeper?"

"I have no way of knowing."

"Is that right?"

"Exactly so."

Wayne shifted around on the bench, looked back to the narrow hallway Edie had gone into, then the gate leading to the platform, finally back to the Storekeeper standing behind the counter.

His tone and expression lost all humor.

"I'm not going, am I?"

"I really don't know," said Storekeeper. "I had been fairly certain that you were. But now, now I just don't know."

What did he mean by that?

"What made you so sure? Before?"

"I couldn't say, really. I just thought you were... needed."

"And I'm not now," said Wayne. "I'm not... needed."

"I don't know," said Storekeeper. "Something has changed. Something is different. I can feel it."

"Right." Wayne leaned back, dropped his hands into his lap. "Me too."

Something caught Storekeeper's attention. Looking to his right, he saw that another train ticket was sitting on the counter. He picked it up, set about to place it into a sleeve.

"It's Molly's."

"I'm glad," said Wayne. "Good for her."

"I believe so," agreed Storekeeper. "I wonder what role she will play, once the train arrives at its destination?"

"Odd you should ask, in just that way. I was wondering the very same thing."

Wayne looked curiously at the Storekeeper.

"What about you, Storekeeper?" he asked. "Will you be going? When the train leaves?"

"No, Mr. Saunders. My own role will play itself out here." Storekeeper admired their surroundings. "My train station. My general store… my world."

"The center of the universe."

"Its very heart." Another look around the station, then he stepped from behind the counter and started toward the gate. "I think I'll give this to Molly. She is no doubt anxious."

Wayne watched Storekeeper walk through the gate and disappear from view. He stood up then, looked about absently and then walked over to the counter, looked casually to where the tickets usually showed up.

Nothing.

"Where'd everybody go?" asked Edie. She was standing near the hallway.

Wayne wandered back toward the bench.

"Out to wait for the train, I expect." He tried to smile, but it was difficult. "Growing impatient, I'll wager."

Edie stepped over to the gate, looked out as she folded her arms. She turned back and looked around the near-empty station.

"But not you?"

"I have yet to be blessed with a ticket."

Wayne climbed up on the passenger bench, sat on the back with his feet on the seat. He clasped his hands together.

"Molly will be going," he said. "He's giving her ticket to her now."

"That's nice," said Edie; *And a relief. What would she have done if Molly hadn't been going?* "Yours will come, I'm sure."

Wayne didn't really think so, but he nodded in response. He stared down at his clasped hands.

"You do remind me of someone, you know… but you're not her."

"I know."

"You are her, but you're not."

Edie moved away from the gate portal, walked over to the bench and sat down at the far end.

"She was a friend of yours?"

"More of an acquaintance," said Wayne.

"And I'm her, but I'm not her."

"The two of you were written different. You came later, I think."

"Wow. That's deep." Edie ran Wayne's comment through her mind a few times. "Very weird, but probably deep."

"That's me. Deep all over." A thin smile came and went. "Now, anyway."

Edie shifted on the bench, turning to look directly at Wayne.

"I do sense the change." A thoughtful pause, then. "The Storekeeper knew me, too."

"The Storekeeper knows everyone who comes to his store."

"But how? We've never met. I'm certain of that." Edie tapped at her temple. "There's a lot missing in here, but I would definitely remember him. He's quite an unforgettable sort."

"True." Wayne slid down from the back of the bench, sat properly. "The Storekeeper knows us because he knows the books we come from."

"Sorry? What?"

Wayne couldn't help but smile at the bewildered expression on Edie's face.

"The woman you reminded me of? She's a dancer. Pretty good one, I guess. She works a club I used to go to when I was living in Chicago."

"Okay… what does that have to do with me? Or with books?"

"She's a character from the book I'm from," said Wayne, quite matter-of-factly. "And you… I'm guessing you're a rework of that same character, only in another book."

"Yeah…" Edie said slowly. "Mr. Saunders, you have totally lost it."

Wayne chose to ignore that, continued unperturbed.

"And Molly… Molly is from a book with no televisions. Will Dawson, he's probably from fifty, sixty years ago; his character has spent a lot of time living in motels while doing whatever it is he does."

"Anthropology," said Edie.

"We're all from different stories, and from different worlds. We know as much as our characters need to know, as much as the writer thought we needed to know." Wayne slid a bit nearer to Edie, looked her in the eye. "The worlds we know are only as complete as our stories needed them to be."

Something about all this was creeping into Edie's thoughts, making her increasingly uncomfortable.

"All right, let's say this is all true. I'm not buying it, you're insane, and probably dangerous, but let's say that everything you're saying is true. So, what are we doing here? How did we miraculously jump out of these mysterious books of yours and show up… *here*?"

"I'm thinking that our writer, our creator I guess you'd call him, is trying to decide which of his characters from earlier books are going to be in his next one." He leaned close to Edie, continued in a faux conspiratorial whisper. "I don't think his books have been all that successful, but he's not ready to give up on his characters."

"So then… you're saying… whenever he decides on a character, a train ticket shows up."

Wayne shifted back, leaned back against the bench. "That's what I'm thinking."

"And the Storekeeper. Is he the writer?"

"I doubt it. No. No, I think…" Wayne thought long and deep. "He's like… the librarian; a miniature librarian living inside the writer's head, keeping track of all his stories and characters and things like that."

"He doesn't know? Wouldn't he know?"

"He's starting to figure it out," said Wayne. "Same as me. Heck, even ol' Mrs. Mayfield is starting to get it."

*Could there be any truth to any of this? No...*

"How did you?" asked Edie. "Figure it out, I mean? Where'd you get all this?"

"Comin' to me in bits and pieces," shrugged Wayne. "More and more as we get closer."

"Closer to what?"

"Ah. Well. For you? Getting on the train, taking it to the final destination; taking on your *'role of a lifetime'*." Wayne looked uneasily away from Edie, down to his tightly clasped hands. "Me? Oh, I figure I'm done."

"No. No, that's not true." It was an automatic response, spoken without really thinking what it all meant. The ensuing silence was powerful. Edie turned away from Wayne, looked across the station, looked at anything but this person sitting on the bench beside her.

*Was any of this true? Could any of it be true?*

"I'm sorry," she said. "I really am."

"Hey, I was in the running for a while." Wayne shrugged one shoulder. "Who knows? Maybe I can head back to Chicago. Maybe hook up with that dancer."

Came then the haunting sound of a distant train whistle…

Wayne and Edie both looked upward, outward.

"That'd be for you," said Wayne. "You better go."

"This isn't right," said Edie. "He can't just…"

"Just what? Not write me into the story?"

"He has to. Now that we're..." She struggled with what all this meant. She was only just beginning to come to terms with it. "We're here now. We're not just characters in a book. We're not..."

She leaned forward and stood then, looked about the station. It was physical. It was here.

"We're *alive*," she said, almost pleading. "I just went to the bathroom, for Christ's sake."

"I'll be all right." A genuine smile from Wayne. "Really."

There was a final, single train whistle, quite near. Wayne looked to the gate. "It's here," he said. "Go on."

Edie looked anxiously from Wayne to the gate. She turned to the ticket counter, started towards it.

"Maybe your ticket is here. Maybe it came late."

She leaned over the counter. *Nothing there.*

Wayne stood.

"Don't worry about me." He moved across toward Edie, took her hand. He guided her toward the gate opening. "Who knows? Maybe I'll see you in the next book."

"Hey, that's right." A sudden sparkle in Edie's eyes. "You said you were in the running for this one. He must like you."

"Absolutely. I figure he just didn't have a part for me in this one." Wayne worked up a confident grin. "He probably has big plans for me in his next blockbuster."

"Yes. I'm certain." Edie felt Wayne let go of her hand. She stepped away. "I'll see you?"

"Absolutely."

Edie gave an uncertain nod, struggled to take another backward step. She turned quickly then, stepped through the gate opening, looked back.

Wayne lifted a hand and held a wave. Edie smiled sadly, turned and was gone.

Wayne stared at the empty gate for several moments more, turned away. He hesitated, stepped finally back into the room. He stopped near the bench, rested a hand on the bench-back. He gazed into the emptiness.

The sound of the train whistle; it rose, then slowly faded, leaving behind silence.

The Storekeeper appeared in the gate opening. Seeing Wayne standing next to the bench, he came into the station and stepped up beside him.

"You should go collect your pennies."

"Pennies?" The word hung there in space, drifted, faded.

Wayne half-turned, spoke without looking at Storekeeper. "Ah. Yes. Pennies... tracks... yes. Maybe later."

Storekeeper looked with some concern at Wayne. "Wayne?"

Wayne breathed in, out, sighed, put on a warm smile. "Wayne…" He thought on that word a moment. Another moment… he shook his head… no…

"Wayne," he said. "Wayne is on his way to Chicago."

"I see," Storekeeper said softly. Realization slowly drifted across his face. "So you are… you are him…"

A slight, easy nod from Wayne. A slow survey of the room, and he indicated their surroundings.

"Quite a nice place you have here," he said. "And I really like your store as well. Very much."

"Thank you. It comes from your second book."

Wayne, now the Writer, smiled comfortably. "Yes. That's right." He indicated the station. "And this… this comes from my first."

"That's right," said Storekeeper.

A warm wave of nostalgia brushed across the face of the Writer. "Oh, I did love that book." He moved around the bench, continued to admire the station as he sat down. "I worked on it for almost three years."

Storekeeper sat down beside the Writer. "And how is the new book coming? I see you have all the characters."

Surrounding sounds began to fade. The world around them slowly grew more quiet, more ethereal.

"It's coming together very well, Storekeeper. Very nice. A good story; the characters are getting comfortable… real nice." The Writer slid back on the bench, leaned back. "It' going to be great. I can feel it. This one… this one is going to be my masterpiece."

"That's good. I'm glad," said the Storekeeper. "And I'm happy for them. They're good people. They are all good people."

The Writer relaxed, rested against the back of the bench. He continued to admire his train station.

"We should head over to the store later," he said. "Get a soda or something."

There was another long pause, then an easy nod from the Writer.

"Ah, Storekeeper… I do love this place."


*~ end*

## The Storekeeper – the stage play

The Storekeeper is a direct adaptation of the three act stage play. The ethereal drama is a full length play with three sets, eight characters.

Printed editions of the stage play, both bound and performance copies, are available through the storekeeper website.

Performance rights are outlined on the storekeeper website.

Please visit:
http://storekeeper.davidrbeshears.com

The stage play has also been adapted to a television screenplay.

Information available at:
http://screenplays.davidrbeshears.com